HAPPY BIRTHDAY, JOSH!

Story by Mary Risk

illustrations by The County Studio

HEINEMANN · LONDON

Inside the cabin of the *Delilah*, Joshua Jones finished his breakfast, and heaved a big sigh. Then he bent down and tickled Fairport under his ears.

"Well, Fairport," he said, "there's no one else around to wish me a happy birthday, so I'll just have to wish it to myself. Happy Birthday, Josh!"

Fairport grinned, and thumped his tail on the cabin floor.

Josh opened the cabin door, and looked down the canal.

"It's a lovely day, anyway," he said, "and birthday or no birthday, I'd better get to work. Admirable Karia's got a load of gravel waiting for me to take up to Biggott's Wharf."

Outside, Fiona Cashmore was just about to call out "Hello!" and knock on the cabin roof, when she heard Josh's voice.

"Oh, so it's Josh's birthday, is it?" she said to herself, and tiptoed quietly away.

As soon as the *Delilah* was chugging on her way, Fiona got busy. She ran to Sharon's mobile café, and rapped on the shutter. Sharon hadn't opened up yet, and was still making sandwiches.

"Sharon!" Fiona called. "It's Josh's birthday, and he doesn't know we know!"

"Well I never," said Sharon. "Josh's birthday, eh? I'll do him a surprise tea. He'll like that."

At home, Mrs Karia was clearing away Wilton Cashmore's breakfast.

"It's Josh's birthday," panted Fiona, "and he doesn't know we know!"

"Oh my!" said Mrs Karia. " I'd better make him a birthday cake!"

Ravi put his head round the door.

"It's Josh's birthday, " said Fiona, "and he doesn't . . . "

" . . . know we know," said Ravi. "I heard you. We must tell Bapu, and Mr Laski, and Daphne, and Spanner! Come on, Fiona!"

At Lock Cottage, the telephone made Admirable Karia jump.

"Yes, yes, who is speaking?" he said. "Oh, number one grandson! Josh's birthday? A surprise? Now let me see . . . "

He put down the receiver and looked round the room.

"The very thing!" he chuckled. "My barometer! It'll warn Josh to batten down the hatches when a heavy sea blows up."

He wrapped up the barometer, and looked out of the window.

"Just in time," he said. "Here comes the *Delilah* now."

"Josh!" he called. "I've got something for you!"
"Really?" said Josh, looking very pleased.
"Yes. I've got a load of gravel to go to Biggott's."
"Oh, I see."
"And this parcel . . . "
"Yes?"
" . . . for Fiona. With the compliments of myself."
"Fiona. I see. Yes, of course, " said Josh.

Joe Laski came rumbling round the corner in his tractor.

"I have here a little parcel," he said.

"For me?" said Josh.

"For you – to give Fiona, please."

"Oh. What's in it?"

"Just something. Please do not shake or drop, Josh. They all can easily break."

Daphne came tooting round the corner in her yellow car.

"Good morning, Josh!" she called. "It's a special day today!"

"Well yes, it is," said Josh. "You see, it's my . . ."

"It's my cow clinic day, " said Daphne hurriedly.

She jumped out of the car and took a parcel out of the boot.

"It's for Fiona, I suppose," said Josh.

"Quite right," said Daphne. "How did you guess?"

"There seem to be lots of parcels for Fiona today," said Josh. "It's not her birthday, is it?"

"Birthday?" said Daphne and Mr Laski and the Admirable all together. "Whoever said anything about birthdays?"

Josh put all the parcels in the *Delilah's* cabin. Fairport sniffed them curiously.

"They're not for us," said Josh. "They're for Fiona."

Fairport whined.

"Oh well," said Josh. "I've got you, and I've got my boat, and I've got loads of friends and . . . Who needs birthday presents? Anyway, I'll celebrate on my own. I'll have two cups of tea with my dinner instead of one!"

Fiona was at home helping Mrs Karia make a big chocolate cake.

"Can I lick the bowl?" she said.

Ravi suddenly appeared.

"Do you need any help?" he said.

"Yes, you can do the washing up," said Mrs Karia.

"I meant help with licking the bowl," said Ravi.

"Oh all right," said Fiona, and together, they finished off the last of the cake mixture.

Soon, a delicious smell was wafting through the flat.
It came out of the kitchen, round the corner and into the
sitting room where Wilton was busy punching holes in
pieces of paper.

He sniffed the air, stood up and followed his nose. It led
him to the kitchen.

"Ah," he said. "Chocolate cake. I'll have some of that."

"Sorry Daddy," said Fiona. "It's for Josh's birthday. What are you going to give him?"

"Me?"

"Yes. Everyone else is giving him a present."

"I see." Wilton Cashmore rubbed his chin. Then he smiled. "I know," he said. "It'll be the classiest present he gets!"

"Good," said Fiona. "Can we ice the cake, Mrs Karia?"

"Do you need – er – any help?" said Wilton.

"No thanks," said Fiona. "Ravi and I can manage!"

"Fiona, what are *we* going to give Josh?" asked Ravi.
   "What about one of those nice pots of flowers we've got on our balcony?" said Fiona.
   "Too big," said Ravi.

"What about a 'happy birthday' badge?"

"Too small."

"Well, why don't *you* think of something?" said Fiona.

"All right," said Ravi. "I will." He thought.

"I know," he said at last. "We'll paint Josh a picture of the *Delilah*, and he can hang it on the wall of the cabin."

"Brilliant," said Fiona. "We'd better get started at once."

It took ages to do the painting, but when it was finished Ravi and Fiona were really pleased with it.

"What do you think, Mrs Karia?" said Fiona. "Honestly?"

"I think it's beautiful," said Mrs Karia, "and I think you'd better wrap it up quickly and take it along to Sharon's. Just look at the time! Joshua Jones will be back with the *Delilah* in less than half an hour."

Down on the wharf Wilton was marching up and down, roaring, "Spanner! Where are you? Dratted boy! Come here at once!"

"We'll tell him you're looking for him," called Fiona.

She followed Ravi round the corner.

"Spanner!" she said. "Daddy's looking for you!"

"I can hear him," said Spanner, "but I'm making a Happy Birthday banner for Josh. How many 'p's are there in 'happy'?"

"Two, I think," said Ravi.

He and Fiona ran on towards Sharon's café.

"Sharon!" gasped Fiona. "It looks wonderful!"

"Thanks love," said Sharon. "I'm pleased with it myself."

"Where did you get the flowers? They look a bit like the ones in the window box outside our flats."

"I don't know. Spanner got those for me. Where is he now?"

"He's making a banner," said Ravi.

"Just like I told him," said Sharon happily. "He can do a lovely job when he tries. All he needs is someone to encourage him."

Fiona helped Sharon put the sandwiches out on the table.

"There's egg and cress, ham and tomato, and cheese and pickle," said Sharon. "And these ones here are my specials."

"What's in those?"

"Potted shrimps and cucumber. Looks a treat, doesn't it? Still, it's a shame we didn't get a birthday cake."

"But we did!" said Ravi. "We made one! And here's my mum bringing it now."

Right behind Mrs Karia was Spanner, trailing a long white piece of cloth behind him.

"Better get that up quick, treasure," said Sharon. "Tie one end on here, to the corner of my shutter, and you can nail the other end to the post over there."

Just then, there was 'toot toot' from down the canal.

"It's the *Delilah*!" shouted Ravi. "Josh's here! Quick, pass the hammer, Spanner. I'll nail up the other end for you."

Funny, thought Josh, looking round the quay. Where is everyone? Where's Sharon's café? Then he saw Ravi and Fiona.

"Hello, Josh," said Fiona. "Had a nice day?"

"Yes, well, " said Josh. "As a matter of fact, it's my . . ."

"Come and have a cup of tea at Sharon's," said Ravi quickly. "She's moved her café round the corner."

"No thanks," said Josh. "There's this gravel to unload, and – oh yes, here are some parcels for you, Fiona."

Just then, Fairport jumped off the *Delilah*, caught sight of Sharon and ran round the corner.

"We'd better go and see what's going on," said Josh.

Josh strode round the corner.
  "Happy birthday!" everyone shouted.
  "Wow!" said Josh. "And I thought . . . How did you know?"
  "Have some tea," said Sharon. "It's on the house today."
  "Fantastic!" said Josh.

"Here are your presents," said Fiona. "From all of us."

"Incredible!" said Josh.

"Blow out the candles," said Mrs Karia, "and make a wish!"

"Well, I'll be . . . This is the nicest birthday surprise I've ever had!" said Josh.

"Oi!" said Spanner. "You haven't looked at my banner yet."

Josh stepped back and looked up. So did everyone else.

"Hippy Barthday to Joshua Jones," he read out loud.

"Eh? What? Hippy . . . ? Oh heck," groaned Spanner. "I must have got all flustered when Mr Cashmore started yelling at me."

"Never mind," said Josh. "It's a great banner, Spanner."

"Course it is," said Sharon. "Go on, Josh, aren't you going to open your presents?"

Josh opened the Admirable Karia's parcel first.

"A barometer!" he said. "What a beauty!"

Then he opened Mr Laski's. Inside were a dozen fresh eggs.

"No wonder he told me not to drop them," Josh said.

Then he opened Daphne's. Inside it was a jar. He read the label. "'Special ointment for sore paws'. No, she's crossed out 'paws' and written 'hands'. Just what I need for my blisters."

"Here's our present," said Ravi. Josh unwrapped it.

"The *Delilah*!" he said. "It's beautiful!"

"Ah, Jones," said Wilton, suddenly appearing. "I believe it's your birthday. I've got a rather special present for you. I'm sure you'll always treasure it. It's a photograph of *me*."

"Well I never," said Sharon, "a present from Wilton Cashmore! Come on, Josh, cut the cake and let's have tea."

"We've got to sing first," said Fiona. "Come on everyone:

Hippy Barthday to you,
Hippy Barthday to you,
Hippy Barthday dear Josh,
Hippy Barthday to you!"

William Heinemann Ltd, Michelin House,
81 Fulham Road, London SW3 6RB

LONDON MELBOURNE AUCKLAND

First published 1992 by William Heinemann Ltd
Joshua Jones film copyright © 1990 S4C
Joshua Jones character copyright © 1989 Rob Lee
Text copyright © 1992 William Heinemann Ltd
Illustrations copyright © 1992 William Heinemann Ltd
All rights reserved
Based on the animation series produced by
Bumper Films for S4C – Channel 4 Wales –
and Prism Art & Design Ltd

ISBN 434 94841 1

Produced by Mandarin
Printed in Hong Kong